The
Night the Reindeer
Saved Christmas

This book is dedicated to Santa's female reindeer
and history's other hidden women.
– Raj Kaur Khaira

A STUDIO PRESS BOOK

First published in the UK in 2020 by Studio Press,
an imprint of Bonnier Books UK,
The Plaza, 535 King's Road, London SW10 0SZ
Owned by Bonnier Books,
Sveavägen 56, Stockholm, Sweden

www.studiopressbooks.co.uk
www.bonnierbooks.co.uk

3 5 7 9 10 8 6 4 2

Edited by Frankie Jones
Designed by Verity Clark

A CIP catalogue for this book is available from the British Library
Printed and bound in the United Kingdom

The Night the Reindeer Saved Christmas

Raj Kaur Khaira

STUDIO PRESS

Kasia Nowowiejska

On a cold winter's day at the very north of the North Pole, Mr Claus was feeling very happy with himself. There was one sleep left until Christmas Eve, and he'd finished all his work.

The presents were wrapped. His suit had been ironed.
The elves had prepared the rockets and the sleigh.
And Mr Claus even set a new record for eating mince pies!

With the hard work done,
Mr Claus decided to relax...

... until a message arrived.

As he read the letter, his heart began to race.

"EMERGENCY MEETING!"

"Everyone in the grotto, NOW!" called Mr Claus.

There was no time to waste.

"Team, I've received some terrible news. The rockets on the Christmas sleigh have exploded. The engineers found tinsel in the thrusters." Mr Claus looked around at his trusted team.

"We can't deliver the presents without the rockets. I'm sorry, but we'll have to cancel Christmas."

"We've been working ALL year!"

"I thought the tinsel would make the sleigh look Christmassy!"

"Think of all the wasted mince pies!"

"The children will be expecting you!"

The elves cried in despair
and Mr Claus shook his head.

But Mrs Claus had an idea.

"There are many creatures that live nearby," she said with a twinkle in her eye. "We should ask them to help us deliver the gifts. Let's spread the word!"

The news of the Christmas crisis spread quickly around the North Pole, carried on the icy winds.

Soon, all the animals lined up to show off their talents and see if they could help.

A pack of polar bears impressed
the judges with their strength...

Z Z Z Z Z z

... until they fell asleep!

"You'd be perfect for carrying heavy gifts!"

"Perhaps you should go back to bed."

"The performance was un**bear**able!"

A pod of narwhals showed off their speed with a race around the bay.

"You could deliver the gifts very quickly!"

"But we don't have waterproof wrapping!"

"I just don't see the point!"

The judges were treated to an aerial display by a flock of kittiwakes.

Next, a troop of arctic foxes performed a magic act...

... and vanished in a
swirl of white snow!

"I need a creature that is as strong as a polar bear and as fast as a narwhal, that can fly like a kittiwake and hide from sight like an arctic fox...

... but I've seen all the animals of the North Pole and no one can help."

But then, through the branches of the trees,
Mr Claus spied something.

Two animals, fast and strong, flew through the sky. Mr Claus
blinked, and they were gone.

"Wait! Come back!" he called, then wondered to
himself "Who could be flying above the trees?"

Mr Claus heard a **crunch** of snow, as two reindeer appeared.

"Blitzen? Comet? You gave me a fright!" he chuckled
"Did you see the creatures flying through the sky?"

"It was us!" replied Blitzen "But we're not meant to fly without the grown-ups."

Flying reindeer! Mr Claus had never heard of such a thing... and he'd lived at the North Pole for a long time.

He followed the young reindeer back to their herd, and was amazed by what he saw.

"I wonder," he said to Comet and Blitzen's father, "would you help me save Christmas by pulling my sleigh across the skies this Christmas Eve?"

"I lose my antlers each winter – all the male reindeer do. I can't fly without the antlers' magic," the big reindeer replied. "But my daughters keep their antlers all year! Perhaps you could ask them."

Mr Claus grinned. Maybe he wouldn't have to cancel Christmas after all.

With just an hour before he had to leave, Mr Claus arrived at his grotto with the eight reindeer sisters.

The elves cheered and Mrs Claus smiled.

The sleigh was soon piled high with presents.

Mr Claus and Mrs Claus helped the reindeer get ready for their journey. It was time to leave.

"Now, Dasher! now, Dancer! now, Prancer and Vixen!
On, Comet! on, Cupid! on, Donner and Blitzen!"
laughed Mr Claus as the reindeer raced across the moon.

"Merry Christmas to all,
and to all a good night!"

It's true, the reindeer that pull Mr Claus' sleigh are female! Male reindeer shed (lose) their antlers in early December, whilst female reindeer keep their thinner antlers throughout the winter season. Female reindeer also cope better with the low temperatures of the North Pole, as they have up to 45% more body fat than males during the winter.

We encounter just a few of the amazing animals that live in the North Pole in this book. Here are some fascinating facts about them:

- Unlike most other bears, polar bears don't truly hibernate. They do, however, spend most of their time resting
- What looks like a unicorn horn on the narwhal is actually a really long tooth
- Kittiwakes are gulls and get their name from their call – "kittee-wa-aake!"
- The fur of an arctic fox changes colour with each season so they can hide easily.